For Found and Lost, with all my love.
Thank you both for deafening wheeks,
contented chirrups, woody flutings, quiver-whiskers,
bright almond eyes and the gift of your days.

BLOOMSBURY CHILDREN'S BOOKS
Bloomsbury Publishing Plc
50 Bedford Square, London, WC1B 3DP, UK
29 Earlsfort Terrace, Dublin 2, Ireland

BLOOMSBURY, BLOOMSBURY CHILDREN'S BOOKS
and the Diana logo are trademarks of Bloomsbury Publishing Plc

First published in Great Britain in 2021 by Bloomsbury Publishing Plc

Text and illustrations © Debi Gliori 2021

Debi Gliori has asserted her rights under the Copyright, Design and Patents Act, 1988,
to be identified as Author and Illustrator of this work.

A catalogue record for this book is available from the British Library

978 1 4088 9291 6 (HB)
978 1 4088 9289 3 (eBook)

1 3 5 7 9 10 8 6 4 2

Printed and bound in China by Leo Paper Products, Heshan, Guangdong

All papers used by Bloomsbury Publishing Plc are natural, recyclable products from
wood grown in well managed forests. The manufacturing processes conform to
the environmental regulations of the country of origin.

To find out more about our authors and books visit www.bloomsbury.com and sign up for our newsletters

Debi Gliori

The Boy
and the
Moonimal

BLOOMSBURY
CHILDREN'S BOOKS
LONDON OXFORD NEW YORK NEW DELHI SYDNEY

I am Moonimal.
This is my story.

Once upon a time,
a boy found me.

He called me
Moonimal and he
hugged me tight.

Moonimals are
made to be
hugged tight.

We were always together.
Boy and Moonimal.
Moonimal and Boy.

Sometimes we were
Moonimal and Explorer Boy . . .

or Moonimal
and Doctor Boy.

We were even Moonimal and Rocket Boy.

We were
Moonimal and Boy.
Forever.

But, one day,
we were playing
in the woods when
Boy tripped and fell.

His glasses broke.
He couldn't see me.
He couldn't find me.

I was lost.

The woods grew dark.

Then light.

There was sun.

Sometimes rain.

Leaves fell.

I waited and waited.

Surely Boy would
come back for me?

Instead, some woodland
creatures found me.

"Three ears!" they squeaked,
"you must be a very special rabbit!"
And they took me
underground to their home.

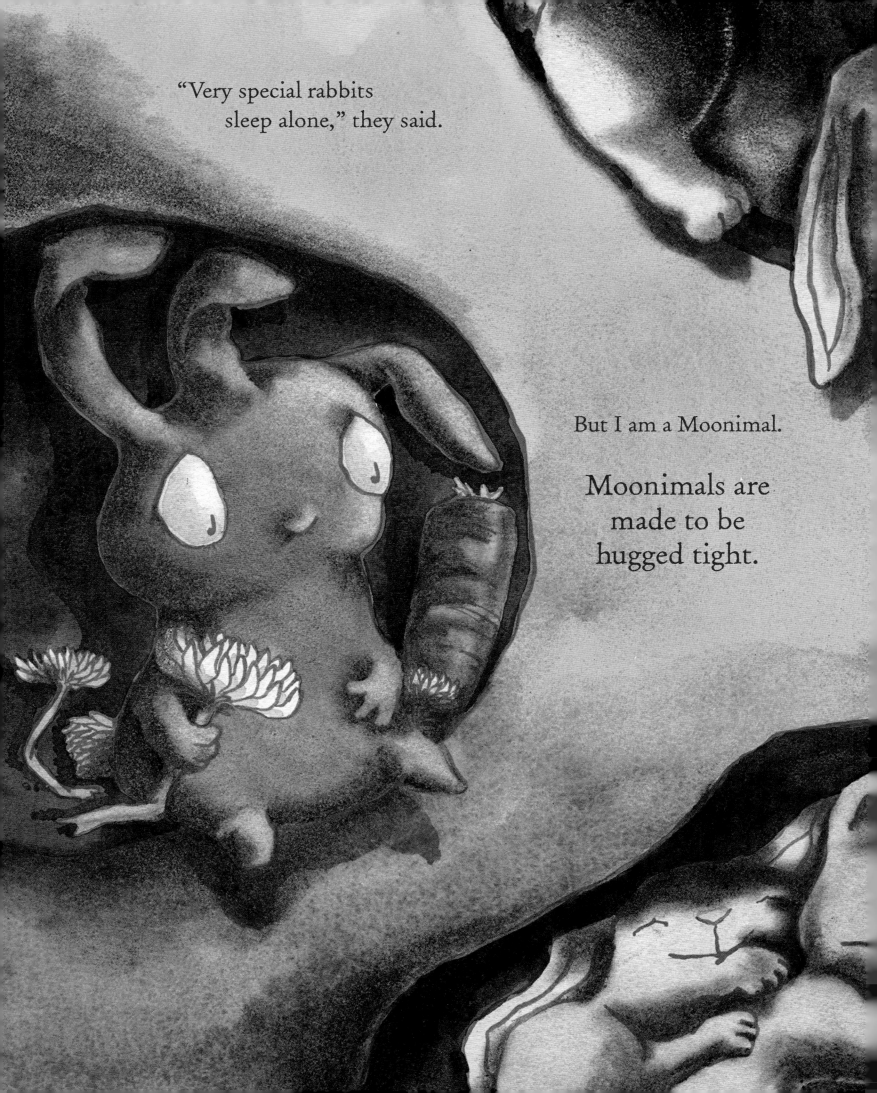

"Very special rabbits
sleep alone," they said.

But I am a Moonimal.

Moonimals are
made to be
hugged tight.

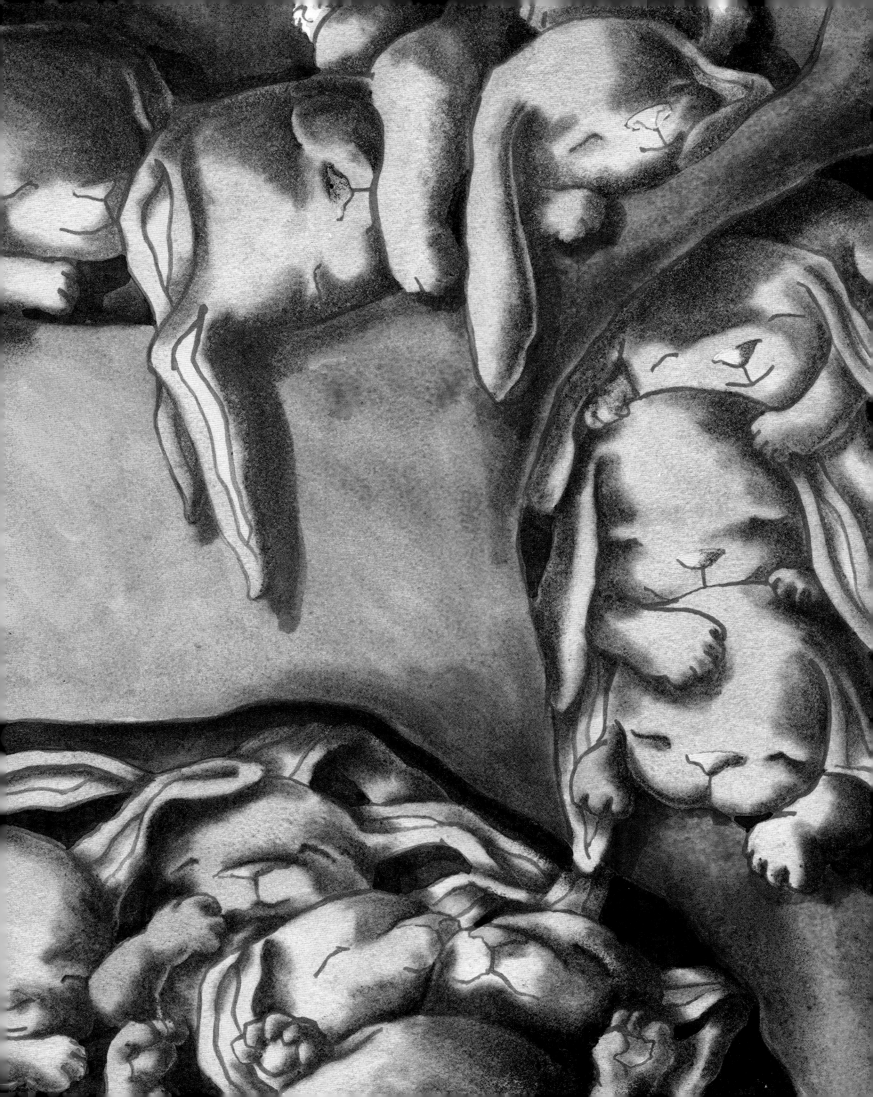

One day, outside in
the carrot field . . .

a thing of wings and
claws lifted me high above
the fields and forests . . .

All the way down.

Straight down

into dark,

cold water.

to where the sky
roared and flashed.

I fell.

The river swept me away.
How would my boy
ever find me again?

Instead, a forest creature found me.
"Such little antlers!" it said.
"You are the smallest King of all."
And he brought me to
his mountain home.

Mountain Kings can see everything in the forest below.
Every day, I looked for Boy, but he never came.

Day by day, year by year, time slipped away.
My coat faded and thinned.

I wondered if my boy
ever remembered his Moonimal.

I would never forget
my boy.

Every winter, we left the
icy mountain tops to find food
in the forest below.

We grazed nervously among the trees,
keeping a lookout for danger.
For many winters, all was well.

Until, one day, danger found us.
The Mountain Kings fled
and, in their haste, left me behind.

I thought my story
was over.

I would never
see my boy again.

He would never find me . . .

"DROP!"
said a voice.

Hands cradled me and raised me high.
Light flashed on glass,
eyes blinked and blinked again.
Then a dear, familiar voice said,

"MOONIMAL!"

My boy!
My very own boy!

I knew he'd come back for me.

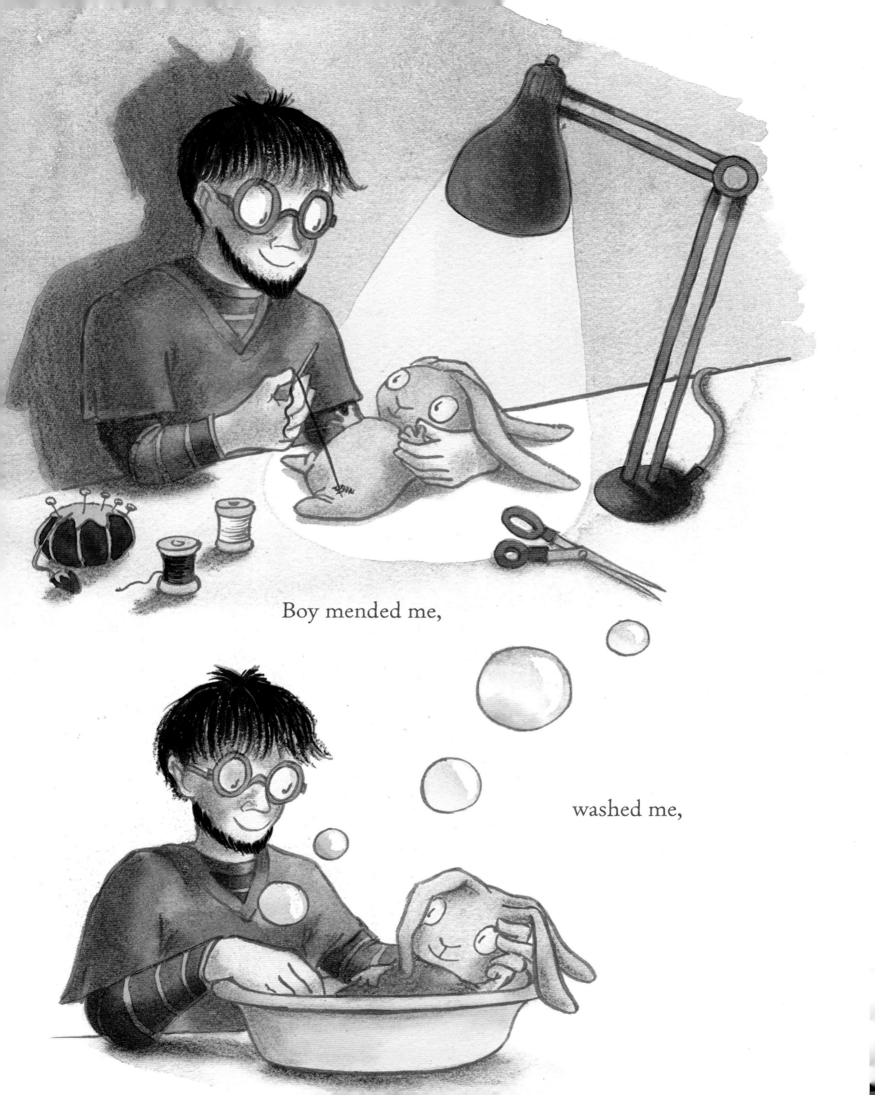

Boy mended me,

washed me,

dried me and hugged me tight.

Moonimals are
made to be
hugged tight.

"Look, Moonimal," said Boy.
"Here is a new story for you."

I am Moonimal.
This is my story.

Once upon a time,
there was a girl . . .